Go-Go's™

CRAZY FOR

CRAZY BONES™

The hot new toy craze!

Go-Go's™

CRAZY FOR
CRAZY BONES™

The hot new toy craze!

BY IZZY BONKERS

SCHOLASTIC INC.

New York   Toronto   London   Auckland   Sydney
Mexico City   New Delhi   Hong Kong

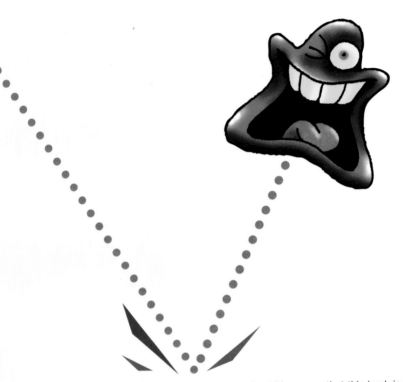

ISBN 0-439-14980-0

12 11 10 9 8 7 6 5 4 3 2 1   9/9 0 1 2 3 4/0

Printed in the U.S.A.
First Scholastic printing, October 1999
Book design: Michael Malone

Play the Craze!

Crazy Bones are the hottest craze to ever hit town because kids everywhere are crazy for Crazy Bones!

Crazy Bones are cool, collectable, wacky characters that come in dozens of colors, shapes, and styles!

They each have their own name...
their own personality...
and **CRAZY** way
of
BOUNCING!

PLAY 'EM...

There's no limit to the number of games you can play with Crazy Bones. Just stir up your imagination...and have fun creating your own crazy games. (But for starters, we've included directions for seven "classic" games on pages 14–20.)

TRADE 'EM...

Trade your Crazy Bones with friends and help one another complete your collections. Just think: One of your friends might have doubles of a wacky character you want. Try to work out a deal. Maybe you can give away something you don't need—and you'll both be happy!

COLLECT 'EM...

This book provides handy lists of the first three Crazy Bones series—"The Go-Go's," "Things," and "Sports," plus a special preview of the newest series, "Buddies." It's fun to try to collect them all. Just think: The rare ones will surely increase in value—hold on to those glow-in-the-dark Eggys!

OUCH! I DON'T MIND THE WOOL, BUT THIS IS RIDICULOUS!

America's newest toy craze isn't exactly, well, new.

In ancient Greece and Rome, kids played a game called Astragals. Nice name, right? Get this: *Astragalis* is a Latin word that means "sheep's knucklebone." To play Astragals, kids needed — yup, you guessed it — a whole mess of sheep's knucklebones.

Kids would clean and dry the bones. They decorated them by painting different faces on the bones. Then they would compete with one another to see who had the best-looking bone. (It was sort of a beauty pageant for, er, *knuckles*.)

But times have changed. Like, sure, sheep's knuckles sound cool and all that. But...YUCK! Gross us out the door! Who wants to walk into a store and plunk down good money for a bag of knuckles? You?

Didn't think so.

So a new toy craze was born. By the way, when children in ancient Greece and Rome threw the bones to the ground, the bones would bounce in all kinds of nutty, wacky, spectacular, *crazy* ways. That's why the modern toys are called Crazy Bones!

FORTUNATELY, WE KEEP OUR BONES...NUMBERED.
Each Crazy Bones character is numbered. What's more, each pack includes free stickers. Collect them all in your own special sticker album!

9

CRAZY BONES
COLOR AND STYLE GUIDE

Glowies

These Crazy Bones actually glow in the dark!

Ice Bones

Transparent in appearance, molded to perfection.

Precious Metals (Gold)

Gold Crazy Bones are extremely rare. In fact, they are considered the rarest among all Crazy Bones to collect!

Sparkles (Not pictured.)

Speckled with silver and gold dust throughout. They are easily recognizable when placed side by side with other Bones.

How many different kinds of Crazy Bones are there?

A lot. *A lot.*

Because each individual Crazy Bone—say, Eggy, for example—comes in a variety of types and colors. There are Glowies and Jellies, Sparkles and Toothpaste, Gooies, Metals, Ice Bones and Whistlers! Here's a quick guide to help you know the difference.

Metals

These metals are considered rare, yet still attainable.

Jellies

Clear, softly colored Bones give a soothing appearance.

Extraordinary Bones (Not pictured.)

Toothpaste
Swirls of colors mixed with streams of pearly white streaks.

Whistlers
Pick up one of these Bones and blow into the hole like a soda bottle.

Gooies
Melted differently into a unique—and gooey—Bone shape.

11

COLLECTOR'S TIP

Probably the most important thing for a collector is to decide what, exactly, you are collecting. You need to narrow the choice. Take coin collecting, for example. After all, you can't collect every coin ever made. So collectors focus on pennies. Or buffalo head nickels. Or, perhaps, all the coins minted in a certain year.

It's the same with Crazy Bones. You can focus on collecting your favorite style of Crazy Bones, such as Jellies or Glowies. Or you could try to get every different kind of a certain character. If "Jaws" is your favorite, why not try to trade for and collect every different type of "Jaws" you can find!

BON

CRAZY QUESTIONS...
QUICK ANSWERS

What are the most difficult Crazy Bones to find?
The gold-plated Crazy Bones are the most rare, because only a limited number of them were made.

Are you going to "bury" or "retire" any Crazy Bones in the future?
As of fall 1999, the Original Sixty have been buried. Also, any Crazy Bone in black, white, or brown has been retired. While you may be lucky enough to still find a few, they are no longer made. Over time, they'll just get harder and harder to find. More Bones will be buried as new ones come on the market.

How many colors are there in all?
We have estimated around 60 different colors.

COWABUNGA!
Surf the Web for Crazy Bones!

Go to the official Crazy Bones Web site at www.crazybones.com. You'll find up-to-the-minute information, including new ways to "Play the Craze!" Plus, you'll find exciting interactive activities and contests offering Crazy Bones prizes.

GET THE REAL DEAL...
Beware of Cheap Imitations!
The genuine Crazy Bones are only made for Toy Craze, Inc. by Magic Box International. Look at the back of your Crazy Bones and you will see the official logo. The logo of Magic Box International is your guarantee that your item is genuine and of the highest quality. Don't be fooled by imitations. Demand the real deal.

13

The Seven Classic Games!

Okay. Maybe you've got a few Crazy Bones. And they sure look cool. But you can't sit there and stare at them forever! Right?! After all, forever is a loooong time. So get up and start playing! Because the best part about Crazy Bones is all the games you can play with them!

Traditional
GAME

1. Each player takes turns to throw or roll five Crazy Bones into the air at the same time.

2. You score points depending on how your Crazy Bones land.

Standing Up (Ace)	5 points
On Side	2 points
Face Up	1 point
Face Down	0 points

3. The winner is the person who scores the most points after three throws.

Which Crazy Bone is right for your game?

You'll find that some Crazy Bones are better for some games than others. For example, some are better for landing on their feet, while others are best for landing facedown. With practice you will notice that the type of ground you play on can change the way that Crazy Bones bounce, and that the large Crazy Bones are best for any of the games where you need to throw them.

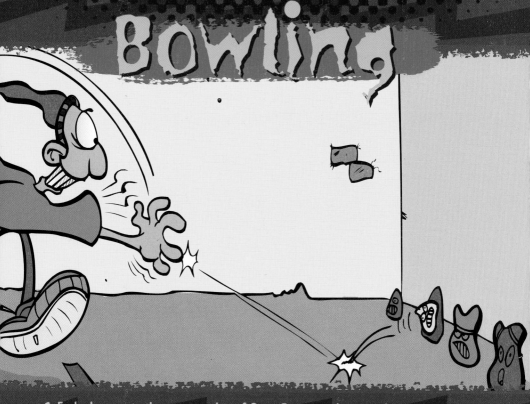

Bowling

1. Each player puts the same number of Crazy Bones on the ground.

2. Place the Crazy Bones approximately six inches from a wall.

3. Each player takes turns throwing a Crazy Bone and trying to knock down as many Crazy Bones as possible. Remember, the Crazy Bones must be thrown, not rolled.

4. Each Crazy Bone you knock down that belongs to another player is worth one point.

5. If you knock over one of your own Crazy Bones, you do not score. Just put it back in its original position.

6. The winner is the player who has the most points after three throws.

Tip: Each player should choose a different color for his "team."

On the Line

1. Draw a straight line on the ground or use a line that is already there.

2. Each player throws a Crazy Bone—no rolling!

3. The player whose Crazy Bone ends up closest to the line is the winner.

4. The game can go on for as long as you like, as long as everyone throws the same number of times. The winner is the player with the most points.

Battle

1. One player lines up six Crazy Bones with a distance of approximately six inches between them.

2. The second player does the same at a distance of about six feet from the other player.

3. Flick a Crazy Bone and try to knock down the other player's Crazy Bones.

4. Remove the Crazy Bones from the battlefield as they are knocked down.

5. Each player takes the same number of turns.

6. The winner is the player who knocks down the most Crazy Bones.

BOMBEr

1. Each player places the same number of Crazy Bones inside a large circle.

2. Players take turns throwing their Crazy Bones from a distance of about six feet, trying to knock the other players' Crazy Bones out of the circle.

3. Each player takes the same number of turns.

4. If by mistake you knock one of your own Crazy Bones out of the circle, it cannot be replaced.

5. If you knock over a Crazy Bone but it does not fall out of the circle, you may stand it up again inside the circle.

6. The winner is the player who has the highest number of his or her own Crazy Bones left inside the circle at the end of the game.

Tip: Each player should use different-colored Crazy Bones to avoid confusion.

Airbone

1. Each player lines up five Crazy Bones approximately two inches apart.

2. Throw the first Crazy Bone into the air and quickly try to pick up the second Crazy Bone and catch the first one before it falls. If you are able to do this, replace the second Crazy Bone and repeat the action with the third Crazy Bone and so on.

3. Next you throw the first Crazy Bone into the air and try to pick up two Crazy Bones at the same time before the first one falls.

4. After that you throw the first Crazy Bone again, and try to pick up a minimum of three Crazy Bones and catch the first one before it falls.

5. When a player makes a mistake another player takes a turn.

6. The winner is the first player who completes the game.

Basket

1. Place a cardboard box on the ground (an empty shoe box works great) about ten feet away from you.

2. Each player takes turns trying to get a Crazy Bone into the box. But... the Crazy Bone must bounce at least once before it goes into the box. If you are really, really good you can decide that the Crazy Bone must bounce two or three times before it goes in.

3. Each player can throw ten Crazy Bones each turn.

4. The winner is the person who gets the most Crazy Bones into the box in ten throws.

USE YOUR CRAZY BRAINS...
AND INVENT YOUR OWN GAMES!

You can create lots of other ways to play with your Crazy Bones. Ask your mom, your dad, or your grandparents for ideas from games they played when they were your age. The number of different games you can play is as limitless as your imagination! Go crazy, and get creative!

CRAZY BONES ™

"The Go-Go's"

Here's the original sixty that started it all, plus a closer look at a few fan favorites! Check off the ones you have!

"The Go-Go's"

 1. MUSIC ☐

 2. SMILEY ☐

3. EGGY ☐

 4. HIPPY ☐

5. VAMPIRE ☐

 6. DAY DREAMER ☐

 7. WEIRDO ☐

8. WOW ☐

9. BIKER ☐

 10. MENACE ☐

 11. PUNK ☐

 12. JUNIOR ☐

 13. BALDY ☐

 14. FUNNY BONE ☐

 15. HEAVY METAL ☐

 16. THE FLY ☐

 17. ROCKER ☐

 18. TOP HAT ☐

 19. RAPPER ☐

 20. SWEETIE ☐

 21. GRUMPY ☐

 22. GHOST ☐

 23. E.T. ☐

 24. GOODIE GOODIE ☐

 25. BONE JOUR ☐

 26. LONG JOHN ☐

 27. BIG MOUTH ☐

 28. CHEF ☐

 29. REGGAE ☐

 30. BABE ☐

22

Play The Craze!

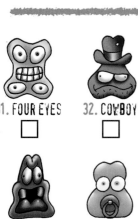

31. FOUR EYES ☐   32. COWBOY ☐   33. JAMES BONE ☐   34. JAWS ☐   35. SCARED ☐   36. FRANKIE ☐

 37. SCREAMER ☐   38. DUMMY ☐   39. CLOWN ☐   40. MONSTER ☐   41. COOL DUDE ☐   42. PIG TAILS ☐

 43. DREAMER ☐   44. SLY BOY ☐   45. JOKER ☐   46. SPEEDY ☐   47. FANG ☐   48. NICE GUY ☐

 49. TEACHER'S PET ☐   50. TUBBY ☐   51. SCARY ☐   52. BRAINS ☐   53. FREDDIE FROG ☐   54. SLEEPY ☐

  55. NEW WAVE ☐   56. BAD BOY ☐   57. DOPEY ☐   58. ANGEL ☐   59. CHUBBY ☐   60. MISS FROGGY ☐

23

NAMED TOP-TEN
FAVORITE FROM
"THE GO-GO'S"

#3

EGGY

NAMED TOP-TEN
FAVORITE FROM
"THE GO-GO'S"

#46

SPEEDY

NAMED TOP-TEN
FAVORITE FROM
"THE GO-GO'S"

#**34**

JAWS

NAMED TOP-TEN
FAVORITE FROM
"THE GO-GO'S"

#**8**

WOW

NAMED TOP-TEN
FAVORITE FROM
"THE GO-GO'S"

#9

BIKER

NAMED TOP-TEN
FAVORITE FROM
"THE GO-GO'S"

#1

MUSIC

26

#18

TOP HAT

#20

SWEETIE

JAMES BONE

COOL DUDE

"Things"

Get a load of a wacky
collection that is really
some "thing" else, plus
a closer look at a few
fan favorites! How many do
you have? Check 'em off!

"Things"

 61. CRAZY BUG

 62. SNIPPY

 63. INKY

 64. MA KETTLE

 65. ARTIST

 66. PSSST

 67. BOOTZ

 68. SPINNER

 69. JAMMER

 70. EDISON

 71. GRAHAM BONE

 72. TWIST

 73. CARMEN BONERANDA

 74. SURPRISE

 75. TOASTY

 76. VEGGIE

 77. CAN CAN

 78. JAVA

 79. BONE BAG

 80. CORKED

 81. MAC

 82. FLASH

 83. CHAMP

 84. COMFY

 85. GIGA BONE

 86. NUTTY

 87. SANDY

 88. CHESTER

 89. SNOOZE

 90. MISS T.

Play The Craze!

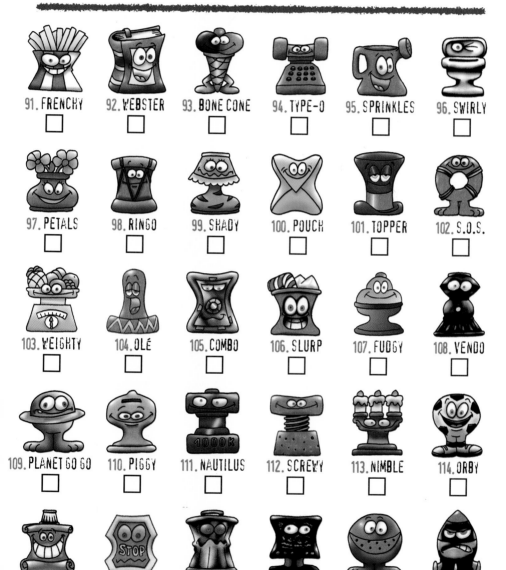

91. FRENCHY

92. WEBSTER

93. BONE CONE

94. TYPE-O

95. SPRINKLES

96. SWIRLY

97. PETALS

98. RINGO

99. SHADY

100. POUCH

101. TOPPER

102. S.O.S.

103. WEIGHTY

104. OLÉ

105. COMBO

106. SLURP

107. FUDGY

108. VENDO

109. PLANET GO GO

110. PIGGY

111. NAUTILUS

112. SCREWY

113. NIMBLE

114. ORBY

115. SQUEEZE

116. OCTO BONE

117. RUBBISH

118. CABLE GUY

119. MELON HEAD

120. NITRO

#120

hiTRO

#85

GiGA Bone

#**96**

SW*iRLY

#**92**

WeBSTER

#91

FRENChy

#81

MAC

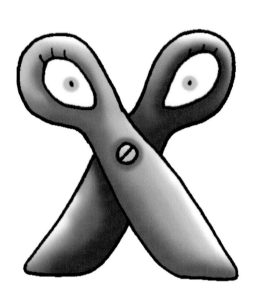

NAMED TOP-TEN
FAVORITE FROM
"THINGS"
#62

SNiPPY

NAMED TOP-TEN
FAVORITE FROM
"THINGS"
#73

CARMEN BONERANDA

NAMED TOP-TEN
FAVORITE FROM
"THINGS"

#109

PLANET
GO GO

NAMED TOP-TEN
FAVORITE FROM
"THINGS"

#113

niMBLe

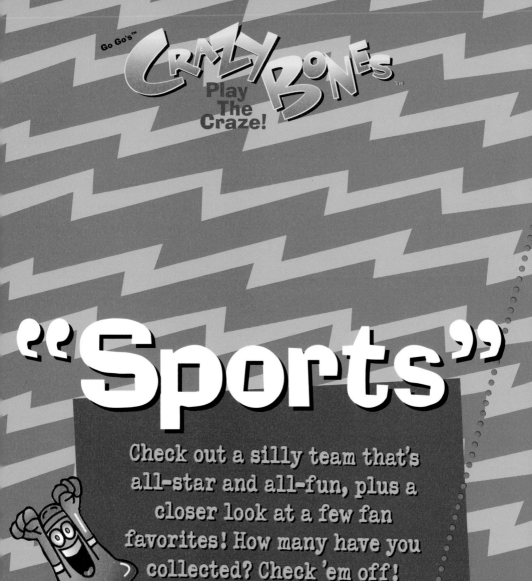

Go Go's™

CRAZY BONES™

Play The Craze!

"Sports"

Check out a silly team that's all-star and all-fun, plus a closer look at a few fan favorites! How many have you collected? Check 'em off!

"Sports"

 1. CHAMP ☐

 2. FLASH ☐

 3. FAN ☐

 4. PLAY BY PLAY ☐

 5. CRY BABY ☐

 6. SCARFO ☐

 7. YIKES ☐

 8. HOORAY ☐

 9. COACH ☐

 10. BANGER ☐

 11. COMMISH ☐

 12. BALL ☐

 13. NET ☐

 14. STRETCHER ☐

 15. CLEATS ☐

 16. CORNER KICK ☐

 17. O.T. ☐

 18. HORN ☐

 19. HANDY ☐

 20. FOOTSKILLS ☐

21. P.K.
☐

22. FREE KICK
☐

23. WINNER
☐

24. MR. COOL
☐

25. THE KID
☐

26. CENTER
☐

27. ROOKIE
☐

28. HEADER
☐

29. DYNOMITE
☐

30. KEEPER
☐

31. TRASH TALK
☐

32. HACKER
☐

33. D·REX
☐

34. CHEAP SHOT
☐

35. WHEELS
☐

36. HEAD CASE
☐

37. NUT MEG
☐

38. STRIKER
☐

39. SILLY
☐

40. SHAG
☐

NAMED TOP-TEN
FAVORITE FROM
"SPORTS"

#**38**

STR★iKER

NAMED TOP-TEN
FAVORITE FROM
"SPORTS"

#**33**

D·ReX

HaCKeR

ROOKie

#9

COACH

#22

FREE KICK

NAMED TOP-TEN
FAVORITE FROM
"SPORTS"

#**26**

CENTER

NAMED TOP-TEN
FAVORITE FROM
"SPORTS"

#**15**

CLEATS

43

NAMED TOP-TEN FAVORITE FROM "SPORTS"

#14

STRETCHER

NAMED TOP-TEN FAVORITE FROM "SPORTS"

#12

BALL

Go Go's™ **CRAZY BONES**™
Play The Craze!

"Buddies"

Here's a sneak peek at the newest set of Crazy Bones — coming soon!

SPECIAL SNEAK PREVIEW!

"Buddies"

 1. TIN MAN ☐

 2. ROBO ☐

 3. ROSEY ☐

 4. STEWIE ☐

 5. SHADES ☐

 6. SQUAT ☐

 7. OVERBITE ☐

 8. OINK ☐

 9. GRAD ☐

 10. PUDGE ☐

 11. PUCK ☐

 12. EEL ☐

 13. STASH ☐

 14. WOOLY ☐

 15. JESTER ☐

 16. HARD HAT ☐

 17. BOWS ☐

 18. TELEBONE ☐

 19. RAZZ ☐

 20. KING BONES ☐

 21. SHERIFF BONES ☐

 22. RASCAL ☐

 23. BIG FOOT ☐

 24. STINKY ☐

 25. BABY ☐

 26. ORBIT ☐

 27. SKIPPER ☐

 28. ZOWIE ☐

 29. NAG ☐

 30. SHARKY ☐

46

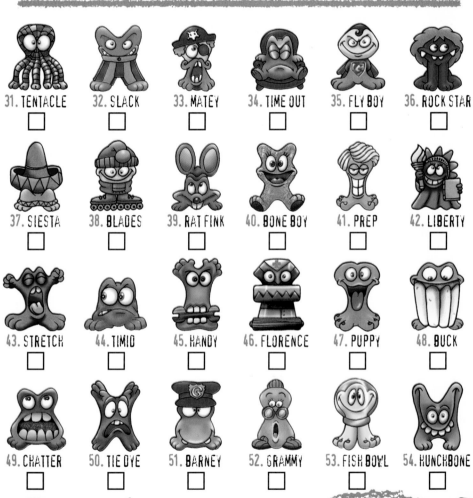

31. TENTACLE ☐

32. SLACK ☐

33. MATEY ☐

34. TIME OUT ☐

35. FLY BOY ☐

36. ROCK STAR ☐

37. SIESTA ☐

38. BLADES ☐

39. RAT FINK ☐

40. BONE BOY ☐

41. PREP ☐

42. LIBERTY ☐

43. STRETCH ☐

44. TIMID ☐

45. HANDY ☐

46. FLORENCE ☐

47. PUPPY ☐

48. BUCK ☐

49. CHATTER ☐

50. TIE DYE ☐

51. BARNEY ☐

52. GRAMMY ☐

53. FISH BOWL ☐

54. HUNCHBONE ☐

55. SLICK ☐

56. HISS ☐

57. HULK ☐

58. BOOKWORM ☐

HEY, COOL! A SPECIAL SNEAK PREVIEW!

WARNING! YOU ARE NOW LEAVING THE BONE ZONE!

THE END

THAT'S THE WAY THE BONE BOUNCES!